LEVEL 4

Re-told by: Paul Shipton
Series Editor: Melanie Williams

Pearson Education Limited
Edinburgh Gate, Harlow,
Essex CM20 2JE, England
and Associated Companies throughout the world.

ISBN: 978-1-4082-8865-8

This edition first published by Pearson Education Ltd. 2013

Eighth impression 2020

Text copyright © Pearson Education Ltd. 2013
Copyright © 2013 Disney Enterprises, Inc. *The Aristocats* is based
on the book by Thomas Rowe. All rights reserved.

The moral rights of the author have been asserted
in accordance with the Copyright Designs and Patents Act 1988

Set in 17/21pt OT Fiendstar
Printed in Great Britain by Ashford Colour Press Ltd.
SWTC/02

Published by Pearson Education Ltd.

For a complete list of the titles available in the Pearson English Kids Readers series, please go to
www.pearsonenglishkidsreaders.com. Alternatively, write to your local Pearson Education office or to
Pearson English Readers Marketing Department, Pearson Education, Edinburgh Gate, Harlow, Essex CM20 2JE, England.

Duchess was a beautiful white cat. She lived in one of the finest houses in Paris with her kittens, Berlioz, Toulouse, and Marie. Their owner, Madame Bonfamille, was very kind. The cats had a wonderful life.

The three kittens were polite to all animals. After they rode home, they always told the horse, "Thank you, Miss Frou-Frou."

Madame Bonfamille asked an old friend, Georges, to visit. He was a lawyer.

"I want to write my will," Madame told him.

From a different room, her butler Edgar could hear Madame's words.

"Her will? I'm going to get all of her money!" Edgar said excitedly. "I'm going to be *rich*!"

"I want my cats to have my money," Madame Bonfamille said. "My butler Edgar must look after them. He can have the money at the end of the cats' lives."

Edgar was not happy. "I don't *want* to look after those cats!" he cried. He had an idea. He got some sleeping pills and put them into the cats' milk.

Edgar brought the milk to the cats.

"Sleep well!" he said. "I mean, *eat* well!"

The cats started to drink their milk.

After a minute, a little mouse came out. Mice are usually afraid of cats, but Duchess and her kittens were friends with all the animals in the house.

"Please eat with us, Roquefort," Duchess told the mouse.

The cats went to sleep quickly. Edgar carried them in a basket to his motorbike outside.

He had a terrible plan. "I'm going to take these cats a long way from Paris and leave them," he said. "With no cats, I'm going to get all of the money in Madame's will!"

He rode through the dark streets of the city.

Duchess woke up to the sound of a storm. "Where am I?"

She looked for her kittens. They were under a bridge. But why?

"I'm afraid," said Marie. "I want to go home."

The family climbed in the basket and watched the rain. "What's going to happen to us?" asked Toulouse. Duchess did not know the answer.

In the morning, Duchess heard the happy sound of a cat's song. It was Thomas O'Malley. He was a cat with no owner and no home.

"What's the problem?" O'Malley asked Duchess.

"I have to go back to Paris," she said.

"I can get you there," said O'Malley. Then he saw Duchess's kittens. "*And* your family!" O'Malley liked the kittens.

O'Malley waited for the next truck to drive by them. He jumped in front of it and the driver stopped.

Before the truck started again, the family of cats climbed into the back.

O'Malley sat in the road and called, "Bye!"

"Goodbye!" cried Marie. But she was not careful and she fell out of the truck.

O'Malley moved quickly. He carried Marie and ran after the truck. He jumped up and then pulled his body into the back.

"Thank you, Mr. O'Malley," said Marie.

O'Malley smiled. He was in the truck now, and it was time for a new plan.

"I'm going to come to Paris with you," he told Duchess.

The cats were in the truck for a long time. Then they had to walk a long, long way. The three kittens were very tired. After many hours, they arrived back in Paris.

But this was not a part of the city that Duchess and her family knew. O'Malley took them to a very different part of Paris.

O'Malley pointed to the top floor of one of the houses.

"We can stay here tonight," he said. "It's quiet."

This was not really true. There were no people in the house, but O'Malley's alley cat friends were all there. Scat Cat and his friends played music late into the night.

After the party, Duchess and O'Malley sat outside under the moon.

O'Malley really liked Duchess. "A father is important for those kittens," he said. "Perhaps you can stay here with me?"

Duchess liked O'Malley, but it was not possible. "We can't leave Madame," she said.

"She's only a *human*," O'Malley said.

"I'm sorry," said Duchess. "We have to go home."

The next day, Edgar the butler had his feet up on the piano. "Those cats are never going to come back!" the butler said happily. "I'm going to be RICH!"

Edgar did not know it, but the cats were outside the house with O'Malley. The kittens ran to their home with Duchess.

"Goodbye," said O'Malley sadly.

The cats were happy – they were home! But Edgar was NOT happy to see the cats again. Angrily he pushed them into a sack.

Roquefort the mouse saw it all.

Quickly he ran outside and shouted to O'Malley. "Help!" he shouted. "You have to help Duchess!"

O'Malley thought fast. "Go and get Scat Cat and his alley cats," he said.

Roquefort ran a long way before he found the alley cats.

They looked at him hungrily.

"A cat sent me for help," cried the mouse. But he was afraid and he could not remember O'Malley's name.

The cats looked *hungrier*.

"Why did I listen to that O'Malley?" cried Roquefort.

"O'Malley?" asked Scat Cat. "Why didn't you say that? Let's go!"

At Madame's house, Edgar carried the sack outside to the stables.

But O'Malley was in the garden. "What's he going to do with Duchess and the kittens?" he cried. O'Malley did not know the answer, but he knew one thing. "I'm going to stop that human!"

Inside the stable, Edgar put the sack into a big trunk.

"You're going to go all the way to Africa!" he told the cats. He closed the trunk and began to push it across the floor. Suddenly, a big cat jumped onto the butler's back — O'Malley!

The alley cat was ready to fight, but Edgar was bigger and stronger.

Suddenly, the door opened and Scat Cat and his friends flew in. They jumped on Edgar and started to fight the butler. The noise was terrible.

Roquefort ran into the stable, too. He jumped on the trunk and started to open it. O'Malley ran to the trunk and helped.

"Come on!" he cried. "Quick!"

"Some stupid *cats* aren't going to stop me!"
Edgar shouted.

But he forgot about one animal – Frou-Frou.

The horse kicked Edgar with her strong legs. He fell into
the trunk. The animals shut the trunk and pushed
it outside.

A truck was there. Two men put the trunk in the back of it.
Edgar was on his way to Africa!

Madame Bonfamille was very happy because Duchess and the kittens were home again. Now O'Malley lived with them, too. This new life in a big, beautiful house was very different from his old life.

But it was not *all* different. Sometimes Scat Cat and his friends came to the house and the cats had the best party in Paris!

Activity page ❶

Before You Read

❶ **Look at the pictures. Read the sentences and choose a or b. What do you think?**

ⓐ  ⓑ

1 Which cat lives in a beautiful house?
2 Which cat is a person's pet?
3 Which cat has no home?
4 Which cat has three kittens?
5 Which cat likes to go from place to place?

❷ **Match the words with the pictures.**

> basket   motorbike   sack   trunk

ⓐ  ⓑ  ⓒ  ⓓ

After You Read

❶ **Number the sentences 1–7.**
  a Duchess and the kittens wake up under a bridge.
  b Edgar falls into the trunk.
  c Edgar takes the cats a long way from the house.

d Edgar puts the four cats into a trunk.

e O'Malley goes back to Paris with the cats.

f O'Malley, Duchess, and the kittens become a happy family.

g Roquefort the mouse gets help from the alley cats.

❷ Read and write True (T) or False (F).

a Edgar is angry because he is not going to get any money in Madame's will.

b O'Malley saves Marie on the road.

c Scat Cat lives with his human owner.

d Roquefort is not afraid of the alley cats.

e A truck drives away with Edgar in it.

f O'Malley joins Duchess and the kittens in Madame's house.

❸ Complete the sentences with the words in the box. Then match them with the pictures.

| angry | afraid | sad | happy |

1 She is _____ because her cats are home again.

2 He is _____ because O'Malley wants to stop him.

3 She is _____ because Edgar is putting her and the kittens into a sack.

4 He is _____ because the kittens are saying goodbye.

 ⓐ
 ⓑ
 ⓒ
 ⓓ